113415
Bc.
Pts

ANTIOCH
"" 2008

D0602249

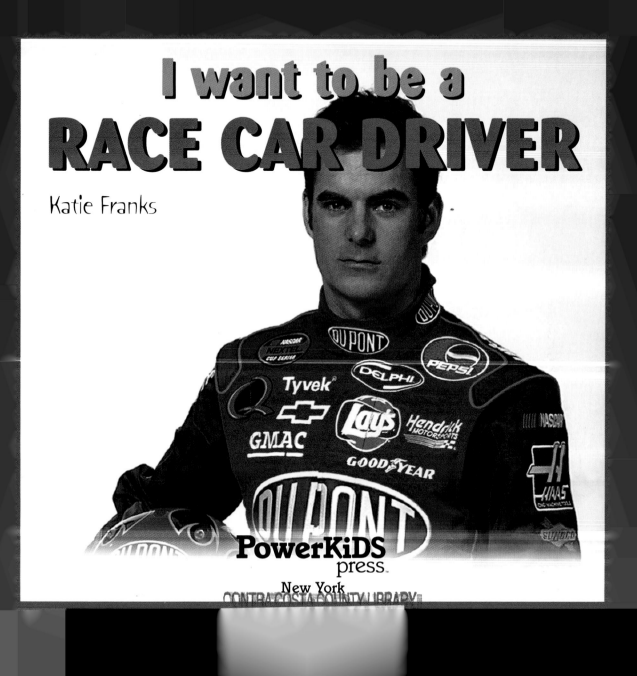

I want to be a
RACE CAR DRIVER

Katie Franks

PowerKiDS press
press

New York

CONTRA COSTA COUNTY LIBRARY

To John, who lives life in the fast lane

Published in 2007 by The Rosen Publishing Group, Inc.
29 East 21st Street, New York, NY 10010

Copyright © 2007 by The Rosen Publishing Group, Inc.

All rights reserved. No part of this book may be reproduced in any form without permission in writing from the publisher, except by a reviewer.

First Edition

Editor: Jennifer Way
Book Design: Ginny Chu
Book Layout: Kate Laczynski
Photo Researchers: Sam Cha and Julia Wong

Photo Credits: All Photos © Getty Images.

Library of Congress Cataloging-in-Publication Data

Franks, Katie.
  I want to be a race car driver / Katie Franks. — 1st ed.
     p. cm. — (Dream jobs)
  Includes index.
  ISBN-13: 978-1-4042-3623-3 (library binding)
  ISBN-10: 1-4042-3623-6 (library binding)
  1. Stock car racing—Juvenile literature. 2. Stock cars (Automobiles)—Juvenile literature. 3. Automobile racing drivers—Juvenile literature. I. Title.
  GV1029.9.S74.F73 2007
  796.72—dc22
                              2006019461

Manufactured in the United States of America

Contents

Jamie McMurray is an up-and-coming race car driver.

Race Car Drivers

Race car driving has become a **popular** sport in the United States. Lots of people watch important NASCAR races, such as the Daytona 500. Do you like to watch car races? Do you have a **favorite** race car driver? Maybe you wonder what it is like inside a race car. This book will show you what a race car driver's life is like, both on and off the track.

Stock cars are made from many brands of
American cars. This is a Dodge stock car.

Stock Cars

NASCAR is a popular type of car racing. NASCAR stands for the National Association for Stock Car Auto Racing. Stock cars are built to look like the cars you see on the street every day.

The first stock cars were made with car bodies and car parts that were available, or in stock, in stores. Now they are built with special parts that help them go faster more safely than a regular car can.

This is the 2006 Daytona 500 race. The Daytona 500 is part of the NEXTEL Cup series.

Types of Races

There are two big **series** of NASCAR races, the NEXTEL Cup and the Busch Series. Drivers often start their racing **careers** in the Busch Series. After a driver has proved himself by racing well in the Busch Series, he might move up to the NEXTEL Cup. This is NASCAR's top series. In NASCAR races the position a driver finishes in gets him a number of points. This is so that the drivers' **rankings** can be tracked.

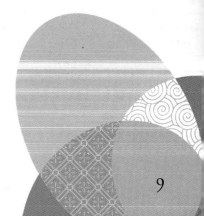

During a 500-mile (805 km) race, a car needs to make pit stops to get more gas. Sometimes cars even change drivers during a pit stop!

Pit Stop

Race car driving is a team effort. During a race the driver will make pit stops.

When a car makes a pit stop, the members of the pit crew rush in to work on the car as fast as they can so the car can continue the race. The crew may change the car's tires or refill the gas. These things can help a car win the race and make sure the driver stays safe.

A race car driver needs to be at the top of his game to drive safely.

Inside a Race Car

A race car driver needs to have the **endurance** for the hard **conditions** during a race. It can be more than 100° F (38° C) inside a racing car! A driver also needs to **concentrate** for hours at a time while driving a car at nearly 200 miles per hour (322 km/h). A driver who is in good shape is better at staying safe from the dangers of the race.

This driver is getting ready to put on his racing helmet.

Race Car Safety

Driver safety is a life-or-death matter in race car driving. High-speed crashes can destroy or flip a car or cause it to catch on fire.

There are many things that help make racing safer. The seat in a stock car is built to help **protect** the driver. It also has a stronger seat belt than a regular car. Drivers are required to wear helmets and special fireproof clothes.

This is driver Greg Biffle signing an autograph at a practice race.

Meeting Fans

During his time off the race track, a driver might have the chance to meet his fans. Sometimes fans get to meet the drivers they like after a race or at special **events**. These fans might ask a driver for his **autograph**. It can also be fun for drivers to meet their fans, because they get to see how much the sport they love means to other people.

KASEY KAHNE FOUNDATION

PAY TO THE ORDER OF ___ *Cornerstone Schools* ___ $ __10,00

_____ 20 ___

Ten Thousand and 00/100 _____ DOL

2005-9

NASCAR driver Kasey Kahne (right) has done charity work for schools.

Charity Work

In their free time, many race car drivers like to do **charity** work. When famous people give their time and money to a charity, their name can bring that charity to the public's attention. This can bring more people and more money to help the charity. A race car driver can also feel good about his charity work because he is helping other people.

In 2006, Jimmie Johnson won the Daytona 500.

The Daytona 500

The Daytona 500 is a 500-mile (805 km) race that is held each year in Daytona, Florida. It is the biggest NASCAR race of the year. People all over the world tune in to watch this race on TV.

The most famous NASCAR drivers race in the Daytona 500, and they are often the winners. The popular drivers Jimmie Johnson, Jeff Gordon, and Michael Waltrip have all won this race in the past few years.

The NASCAR Hall of Fame

In 2006, Charlotte, North Carolina, was picked to be the location of the NASCAR Hall of Fame. The first NASCAR race was run in Charlotte.

The Hall of Fame will be a **museum** that houses objects from the history of stock car racing. It will also honor racing **legends**. When the Hall of Fame opens in 2010, fans and drivers alike will feel proud to have a place that honors one of the fastest-growing sports.

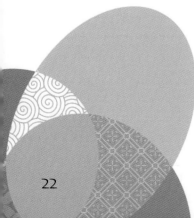

Glossary

autograph (AH-toh-graf) A person's name, written by that person.

careers (kuh-REERZ) Jobs.

charity (CHER-uh-tee) A group that gives help to the needy.

concentrate (KON-sen-trayt) To direct one's thoughts and attention on one thing.

conditions (kun-DIH-shunz) The ways people or things are, or the shape they are in.

endurance (en-DUR-ints) Being strong and going long distances without getting tired easily.

events (ih-VENTS) Things that happen, often planned ahead of time.

favorite (FAY-vuh-rut) Most liked.

legends (LEH-jendz) People who have been famous and honored for a very long time.

museum (myoo-ZEE-um) A place where art or historical pieces are safely kept for people to see and to study.

popular (PAH-pyuh-lur) Liked by lots of people.

protect (pruh-TEKT) To keep safe.

rankings (RAN-kingz) Measures of how well a player is doing in a sport.

series (SIR-eez) A group of like things.

Index

Web Sites

Due to the changing nature of Internet links, PowerKids Press has developed an online list of Web sites related to the subject of this book. This site is updated regularly. Please use this link to access the list:

www.powerkidslinks.com/djobs/racecar/